SILVER PENNY STORIES

The Three Little Pigs

Told by Diane Namm

Illustrated by Scott Wakefield

Once upon a time, in a tiny cottage, there lived three very different little pigs.

Mother Pig did her best to take care of them. Until one day, . . .

. . . the Smartest Pig said, "Mother, it is time for us to leave and build our own homes."

The Lazy Pig and the Not-So-Very-Clever Pig did not want to leave. But at last they agreed.

Mother Pig kissed them goodbye.

The three little pigs came to
a crossroads.

"I will build right here," said the
Lazy Pig.

"I will build right there," said the
Not-So-Very-Clever Pig.

"I will build way up there," said the
Smartest Pig, pointing to the top of
a hill.

"Brothers," said the Smartest Pig,

"work hard and build strong houses.

And remember the Big Bad Wolf."

"Fiddlesticks!" said the other two.

"We don't care about him!"

The three little pigs went their separate ways.

The Lazy Pig built his house of straw.

The Not-So-Very-Clever Pig built his house of sticks.

And the Smartest Pig built his house of bricks.

"Time for sleep!" yawned the
Lazy Pig.

"Time for games!" laughed the
Not-So-Very-Clever Pig.

"Time for dinner," said the
Smartest Pig.

So he made a fire and put a stew
pot on to boil.

Along came the Big Bad Wolf. He saw the Lazy Pig's house of straw.

He grinned a wolfish grin. He knocked on the door and sang, "Little pig, little pig, let me in!"

"Not by the hair of my chinny-chin-chin," said the Lazy Pig.

"Then I'll huff and I'll puff and I'll blow your house down," said the Big Bad Wolf.

And that's what he did.

The Lazy Pig ran to his brother's house of sticks.

"The Big Bad Wolf huffed and puffed and blew my house down!" squealed the Lazy Pig. "And he's on his way here!"

Along came the Big Bad Wolf. He saw the Not-So-Very-Clever Pig's house of sticks.

He grinned a wolfish grin. He knocked on the door and sang, "Little pig, little pig, let me in!"

"Not by the hair of my chinny-chin-chin," said the Not-So-Very Clever Pig.

"Then I'll huff and I'll puff and I'll blow your house down," said the Big Bad Wolf.

And that's what he did.

The Lazy Pig and the Not-So-Very-Clever Pig ran to their brother's house of bricks.

"The Big Bad Wolf huffed and puffed and blew our houses down," they squealed. "And he's on his way here!"

Along came the Big Bad Wolf.
He saw the Smartest Pig's house
of bricks.

He grinned a wolfish grin. He
knocked on the door and sang,
"Little pig, little pig, let me in!"

"Not by the hair of my chinny-chin-chin," said the Smartest Pig.

"Then I'll huff and I'll puff and I'll blow your house down," said the Big Bad Wolf.

So he huffed and he puffed. He puffed and he huffed.

But the Big Bad Wolf could NOT blow down the house of bricks.

"Ha-ha!" the pigs laughed. "No way in. Not by the hairs of our chinny-chin-chins."

"The wolf is gone!" the little pigs sang.

The Smartest Pig said, "I've made stew for dinner! Let's eat!" He headed for the boiling stew pot on the fire.

But the Big Bad Wolf circled
the house.

He looked down. He looked up.
He grinned a wolfish grin.

The Big Bad Wolf crawled up onto
the roof and climbed down into
the chimney . . .

. . . just as the Smartest Pig uncovered the boiling pot.

Down, down, down went the wolf into the chimney.

Suddenly, there was a . . .

. . . SPLASH and a HOWL!

The Big Bad Wolf dropped right into the boiling pot.

"Help me out! Help me out!"
the Big Bad Wolf shouted.

"Not by the hairs of our chinny-chin-chins!" sang the pigs.

Instantly, the Smartest Pig covered the pot.

The three little pigs had wolf stew to last them for a month.

And they lived happily ever after in the sturdy house of bricks.

STERLING CHILDREN'S BOOKS
New York

An Imprint of Sterling Publishing
387 Park Avenue South
New York, NY 10016

STERLING CHILDREN'S BOOKS and the distinctive Sterling Children's Books
logo are trademarks of Sterling Publishing Co., Inc.

© 2012 by Sterling Publishing Co., Inc.
Design by Jennifer Browning

ISBN 978-1-4027-8434-7

Library of Congress Cataloging-in-Publication Data Available

Distributed in Canada by Sterling Publishing
c/o Canadian Manda Group, 165 Dufferin Street
Toronto, Ontario, Canada M6K 3H6
Distributed in the United Kingdom by GMC Distribution Services
Castle Place, 166 High Street, Lewes, East Sussex, England BN7 1XU
Distributed in Australia by Capricorn Link (Australia) Pty. Ltd.
P.O. Box 704, Windsor, NSW 2756, Australia

For information about custom editions, special sales, and premium and corporate
purchases, please contact Sterling Special Sales at 800-805-5489
or specialsales@sterlingpublishing.com.

Printed in China
Lot #:
2 4 6 8 10 9 7 5 3 1
07/12

www.sterlingpublishing.com/kids